MW01047770

AVERNE

PUBLISHING COMPANY

Dedication

This book is dedicated to all the women, mothers, daughters, and little girls around the world. We all have a little Margarette in us and she represents happiness in childhood. Thanks to all who inspired me and help me through my journey. Look forward to more adventures with Margarette in the future.

STORY

It's June 1, 1987, the last day of school and boy am I excited. As Margarette leaves class her long braids hanging down her back bouncing with each step she takes.

Margarette walked down the hall talking to her friend Valerie. She tells her "today marks the start of my favorite time of year, the summer vacation."

The summer means so much to me because I get to go to my granny's house, down south during the break. Granny is very special to me she always lets me help her pick tomatoes, cucumbers and fat watermelons out of her beautiful garden.

Granny loves to have me in the kitchen right beside her, as we prepare dinner together. I like when she makes my favorite dish, fried chicken, homemade biscuits with gravy and rice. It smells good and taste even better.

I can't wait to get home because my suitcase has been packed for the last two days already and mommy said, "we will be driving to granny's when I get home from school." I always pack a lot of pink, its Granny's favorite color so we match.

The bus ride home seemed to take forever, I sat in my seat daydreaming of the fun summer ahead.

The bus finally pulled up to my house and I dashed through the door.

My mommy was at the front door to welcome me home. I kissed her on the cheek and rushed up to my room to get my suitcase.

I came down the stairs with my suitcase and mom said, "hold your horses Margarette: you haven't even had your snack yet."

My mommy always makes the best snacks and today I got a peanut butter and jelly sandwich with animal crackers and a juice box.

I finished, and mommy took my suitcase and put it in the trunk of the car. I felt good because the journey to granny's was about to begin. When going to granny's house I always get to ride in the front seat, so I opened the car door sat down and buckled up.

My mommy lets me listen to whatever I want on the radio while she drives. I turned on the radio and my mommy started to sing with the song that was playing, I had never heard it before, but I liked the beat because It made me close my eyes and relax. I must have fell asleep, because when I opened my eyes again, mommy said "Margarette we are at granny's house."

It was dark outside, but granny came to the car to give me a big kiss and squeezed my cheeks, like she always does.

1214

My granny was beautiful with her long curly hair, blowing in the wind and bright color dress. She reminded me of a movie star I once saw on tv.

I couldn't wait to get inside granny's house to put on my pajamas and tell granny about my last day at school. She always liked my stories and laughed at my jokes. Every night before I went to bed, granny would give me cookies and a glass of warm milk before we said our prayers.

The next morning granny was busy in the kitchen, you could smell the bacon and scrambled eggs, the aroma was coming into my room. My granny always made a big breakfast because she wants my tummy to be full before I start my day.

I have a lot of friends around my granny's neighborhood that I play with daily, until granny needs my help with dinner. My best friends from granny's neighborhood were Shirley and Shannon and we love to jump rope together.

As I opened the front door they were heading to see if I could come out and play. I had a kool-aid smile on my face because I had not seen them since last summer.

We shared hugs and kisses then granny said "you girls go have fun."

We all ran to the front yard where Shannon had a brand new clothes line that we used as our jump rope.
It is so amazing how when you enjoy jumping rope with your friends the time seems to pass by quickly.

My granny called me inside for dinner because the sun started to go down. I said "goodnight" to my friends and headed inside.

When I opened the door I could tell dinner was almost ready. My granny told me to go wash up and come back to help her set the table. I joyfully went upstairs to take a bath and put on my sparkly pink floral pajamas.

Margarette came down and asked granny "where she put the placemats?" Granny showed me and I put them neatly on the table with forks, spoons and cups. The way I set the table made granny's eyes light up because she showed me last summer and I didn't forget how to do it. We said our grace over the food and began to enjoy the steak, mashed potatoes with carrots and a tall glass of lemonade.

26

After my tummy was filled, I had a smile on my face. Granny took my hand and walked me upstairs to my room. We said our prayer together on our knees by the side of the bed.

She tucked me in and kissed my forehead. As grandma was leaving she looked back at me and said I love you and turned the light out.

Made in the USA
Middletown, DE
13 December 2024

66777571R00018